GW00865938

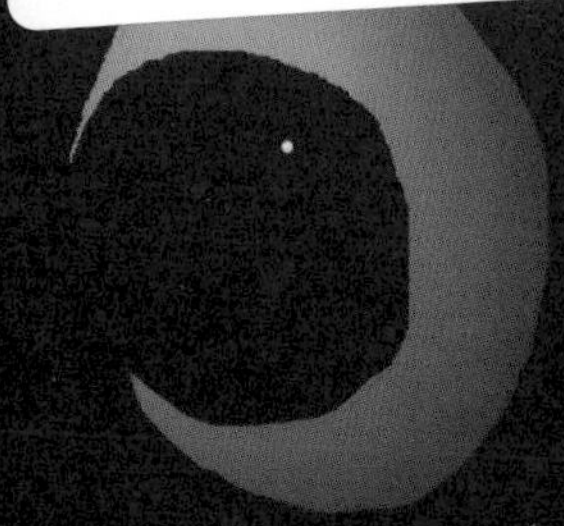

DARE TO BE DIFFERENT

The series 'Dare To Be Different' aims to educate children and promote a feeling of inclusion.
Dare To Be Different is a series of stories aimed at helping children understand that it's OK to be an individual.
In the Dare To Be Different books, each character overcomes their own problem, enabling children to manage issues that might affect their lives such as food allergies, other health conditions or different beliefs.

Titles coming up under Dare To Be different series : Nutty The Squirrel, Patrick The Pony, Morag The fussy Goat....

Concept &
Layout Designer
Maini Singh

Writer
Michelle Eshkeri

Illustrator
Juliette Najman

Backgrounds Designer
Bettinal Fernandez

Editor
Peter Larkin

First published in 2020, London, United Kingdom.

This book belongs to

____

Another day and another night,
Pete could not sleep, try as he might.

He lay in his bed with his eyes open wide,
sleep wouldn't come no matter how hard he tried.

He looked all around, and it made him insane,
his family lay sleeping as he tugged at his mane.

Pete had never had this trouble before,
but recently, it was happening more and more.

He got up again and walked round the den,
'I'll trot about some more and maybe then...

I'll feel a bit sleepy and crash right out'
said Pete to himself, 'cos no-one else was about.

But that didn't work, so he got himself a drink,
hot milk makes you sleepy, so they think.

But the milk didn't help, now he needed to wee,
so he got up again and crossed over to the tree.

Maybe the lavender would help him sleep,
he was so tired now, he wanted to weep.

The morning arrived; everyone was snoring,
life on his own was dreadfully boring.

He'd tried turning off the light on his tablet too,
he'd heard bad things about lights that were blue.

He didn't drink coffee or eat sugary stuff,
nothing helped him sleep, it was getting so tough.

Next night in despair, he tore up his bed
to find a comfy place to lay his head.

'Oh, wait, what's that?' said Pete, with a groan,
under his bed, he found a leftover bone.

'A leftover bone is what's caused all this stress!
Just a simple bone turned me into a mess.'

So now Pete keeps his space nice and clean...
and has most of the time to dream and dream.

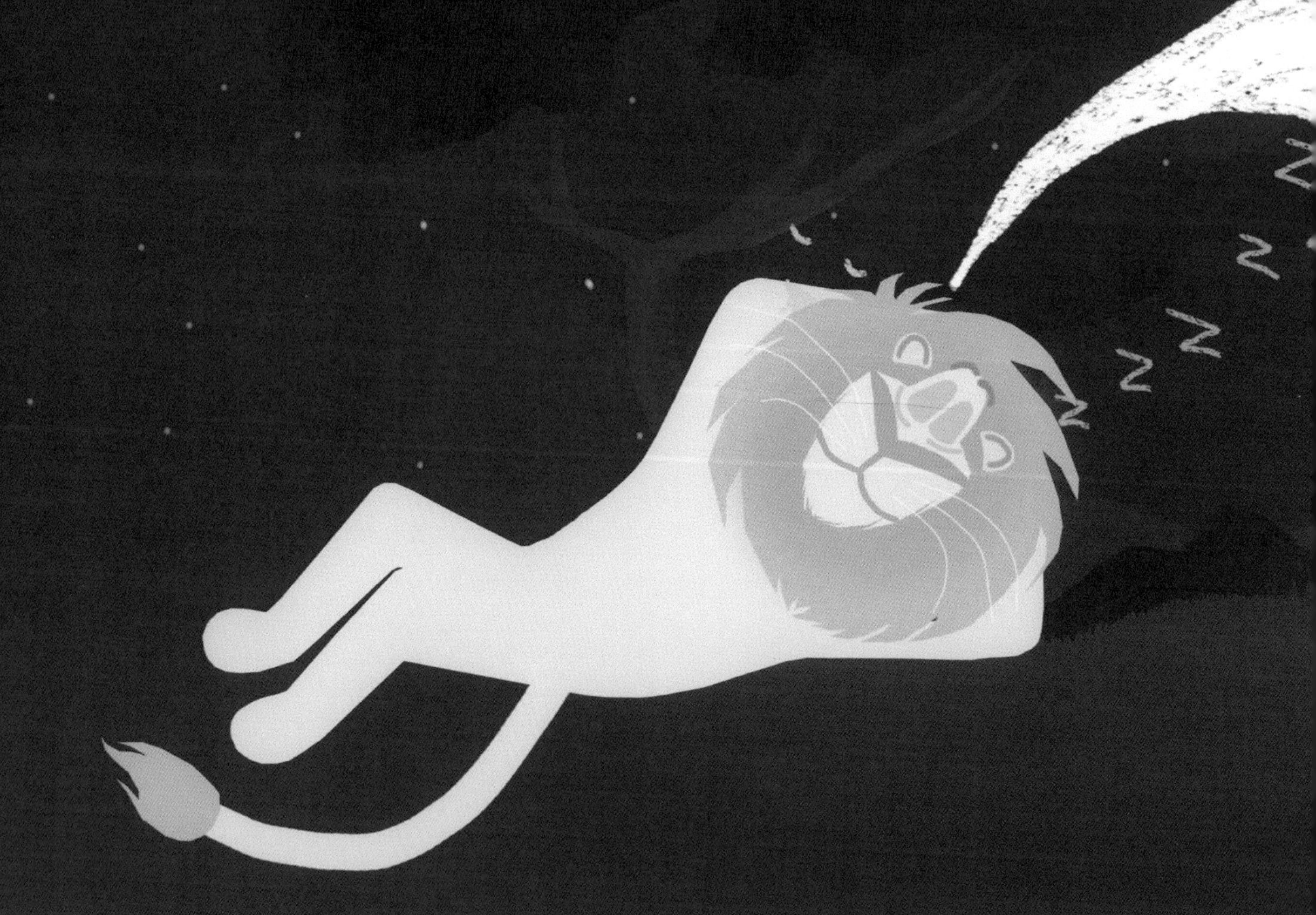

Colour in your own Pete...

Printed in Great Britain
by Amazon

67381534R00015